Birthday Parties

Characters

 **Red Group**

 **Blue Group**

 **Purple Group**

 All

Setting Different homes

by Francisco Blane

My Picture Words

birthday party

cake

candy

pizza

My Sight Words

have	he
like	she
we	will

 He is 6.

 We will have .
cake

 We like the .
cake

 She is 7.

 We will have .
cupcakes

 We like the .
cupcakes

 She is 8.

 We will have 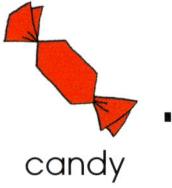.
candy

 We like the 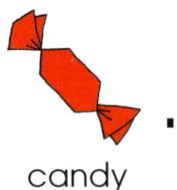.
candy

 He is 9.

 We will have 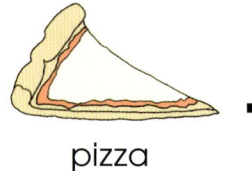 .
pizza

 We like the  .
pizza

 We like the  !

birthday party

The End

Birthday Parties

Characters

 **Red Group**

 **Blue Group**

 **Purple Group**

 All

Setting   Different homes

by Francisco Blane

My Picture Words

birthday party

cake

candy

pizza

My Sight Words

have	he
like	she
we	will

 He is 6.

 We will have .
cake

 We like the .
cake

 She is 7.

 We will have .
cupcakes

 We like the .
cupcakes

 She is 8.

 We will have 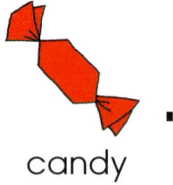.
candy

 We like the .
candy

 He is 9.

 We will have 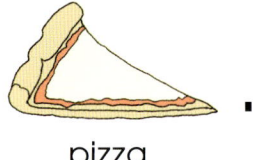.
pizza

 We like the .
pizza

 We like the  !
birthday party

The End

Birthday Parties

Characters

 **Red Group**

 **Blue Group**

 **Purple Group**

 All

Setting Different homes

by Francisco Blane

My Picture Words

birthday party

cake

candy

pizza

My Sight Words

have	he
like	she
we	will

 She is 8.

 We will have 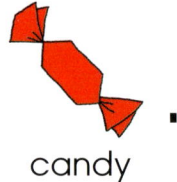.
candy

 We like the 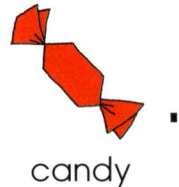.
candy

 He is 9.

 We will have  .
pizza

 We like the  .
pizza

 We like the  !

birthday party

The End